Oliver Optic

Careless Kate

A Story for Little Folks

Oliver Optic

Careless Kate
A Story for Little Folks

ISBN/EAN: 9783744771115

Printed in Europe, USA, Canada, Australia, Japan

Cover: Foto ©Andreas Hilbeck / pixelio.de

More available books at **www.hansebooks.com**

THE RIVERDALE BOOKS.

CARELESS KATE.

A STORY FOR LITTLE FOLKS.

BY

OLIVER OPTIC,

AUTHOR OF "YOUNG AMERICA ABROAD," "THE ARMY AND NAVY SE-
RIES," "THE WOODVILLE STORIES," "THE STARRY FLAG SERIES,"
"THE BOAT CLUB STORIES," "THE LAKE SHORE SERIES," "THE
UPWARD AND ONWARD SERIES," "THE YACHT CLUB
SERIES," "THE GREAT WESTERN SERIES," ETC.

BOSTON 1889
LEE AND SHEPARD PUBLISHERS
10 MILK STREET NEXT "OLD SOUTH MEETING HOUSE"
NEW YORK CHARLES T. DILLINGHAM
718 AND 720 BROADWAY

S. J. PARKHILL & CO., PRINTERS, 222 FRANKLIN STREET, BOSTON.

CARELESS KATE.

I.

"KATE!" said Mrs. Lamb to her daughter, who was playing in the garden, in front of the house.

"What do you want, mother?" replied the little girl, without even lifting her eyes from the ground, in which she was planting a marigold.

I don't think any of my young readers regard this as a proper answer for a little girl to make to her mother; and I hope none of them ever speak to their parents in this manner.

"Come into the house. I want you," added her mother.

But Kate did not go till she got ready. She was not in the habit of minding her mother at once, and without asking any improper questions as, all good children do, or ought to do, at least.

When she stepped out of the bed of flowers, in which she had been at work, instead of looking to see where she put her feet, she kept her eyes fixed on the place where she had just planted the marigold.

" Look before you leap " is a good motto for everybody — for children, as well as for men and women.   If Kate had thought of it, perhaps she would have saved herself and her mother a great deal of trouble.

She did not mind where she stepped, and put her foot upon a beautiful, sweet-scented peony, which had just come out of the ground. She broke the stem short off, and crushed the root all in pieces.

Now, this flower was very highly prized by Mrs. Lamb, for she had brought it from a great distance, and it was the only one of the kind in Riverdale at that time.

Kate was very fond of flowers herself, and when she saw the mischief she had done, she cried with anger and vexation. She would not have spoiled this peony for a great deal, for she had looked forward with much pleasure to the time when it should bud and blossom, and fill the garden with its fragrance.

"What is the matter with you, Kate?" called her mother, from the house, when she heard Kate crying.

"I did not mean to do it, mother," sobbed the poor girl.

"Didn't mean to do what, Kate?" said her mother, rushing into the garden to find out what mischief had been done.

Mrs. Lamb was very angry when she saw that the peony was spoiled; and she took

Kate by the arm, and shook her. I don't think this shaking did any good; but it was a great trial to her to see her favorite flower destroyed.

"You careless girl!" said Mrs. Lamb.

"I didn't mean to, mother," replied Kate.

"But you were careless, as you always are. Will you never learn to be careful? You walk about the flower beds as though they were solid rocks."

"I did not mean to tread upon it," was all that poor Kate could say.

It was very true that she did not mean to spoil the peony; but it was almost as bad to ruin it by being careless. Children ought to understand that not meaning to do wrong is not a good excuse, when the wrong might have been prevented by being careful.

Suppose the captain of a

ship should run his vessel on the rocks, and lose a dozen lives, by being careless; do you think people would be willing to trust him with another vessel afterwards?

Suppose the engineer should neglect to keep watch of the boiler, and it should burst; would not people blame him? Would they think it a good excuse if he said he did not mean to let it burst?

If the man who has the keeping of a powder house should smoke a pipe in it, and twenty persons should be killed by his carelessness, do you think it would be enough for him to say he did not intend to kill them?

When we go on the water in a sailing vessel or a steamer; when we ride on a railroad, in a stage, or wagon, our lives depend on the carefulness with which the vessel, railroad, or carriage is managed. People don't excuse them, when lives are lost, because they did not mean to kill anybody.

You are liable to lose your life every day by the carelessness of some one. The house in which you are to sleep on a cold winter's night may be burned down by the neglect of those who take care of the fires.

The careless use of a lamp

might destroy many lives and much property. If you play with fire, though you do not mean any harm, you may burn the house in which you live, and perhaps destroy the lives of your friends.

A little carelessness may produce dreadful results. The want of thought for a few moments may do more mischief than you can repair in a whole lifetime.

Kate Lamb was not a bad

girl at heart. She loved her parents and her friends as much as any little girl; but she often gave them a great deal of trouble and sadness by her carelessness.

She was so thoughtless that she had come to be called "Careless Kate." It was a bad fault; and it sometimes led her to commit worse ones, as my story will show.

"Now, Kate, come into the house; and next time, when

I call, come at once," said her
mother. "If you had minded
me, perhaps my flower would
not have been spoiled."

"I will be more careful
next time, mother," replied
Kate.

"I hope you will. I think
you have done sufficient mischief by being careless, and I
hope you will soon begin to
do better."

"I will try, mother."

Very likely she meant to

try, just then, while she was
smarting under her mother's
rebuke, and while she was
still sad at the loss of the
flower; but she had promised
to do better so many times,
that her mother could hardly
believe her again.

"I want you to carry this
quart of milk down in the
meadow to poor Mrs.
O'Brien," said Mrs. Lamb,
as she handed her a tin kettle. "And you must go

quick, for it is almost dark now."

"It won't take me long, mother."

"But you must be very careful, and not spill any of the milk."

"I will be very careful."

"Mrs. O'Brien is sick, and has two small children. This milk is for their supper."

"That is the woman whose husband was killed on the railroad last summer — isn't it, mother?"

" Yes; and she is very poor. She is sick now, and not able to work. The neighbors have all sent milk to her for her children, and a great many other things. Now go just as fast as you can, but be very careful and not spill the milk."

MRS. O'BRIEN AND HER CHILDREN.

II.

KATE put on her bonnet, and taking the pail of milk, hastened towards the house of the poor sick woman. But she had gone but a little way when she met Fanny Flynn, who was an idle girl, and very fond of mischief.

"Where are you going, Kate?" asked Fanny.

"I am going down to Mrs. O'Brien's with some milk."

"Give me a drink — will you?"

"I can't; it is for the poor widow's children. I suppose they won't have any supper till they get this milk."

"Yes, they will. I won't drink but a little of it."

"No, I can't give you any. It would not be right for me to do so."

"Pooh! You needn't pretend to be so good all at once. You are no better than I am."

"I didn't say I was. Only I shall not give you any of this milk, when it is for the poor woman's children; so you needn't ask me," replied Kate, with a great deal of spirit.

Some people think, when they do any thing that is right, they ought to make a great parade over it; but this only shows that they are not much in the habit of doing right, and they wish to get all the credit they can for it.

It was so with Kate. She ought to have been content with merely doing her duty, without "talking large" about it. Fanny felt that she was just as good as Kate, and she was angry when the latter made a needless show of her intention to do what she believed to be right.

"I don't want it," said Fanny.

"What did you ask me for it for, then? You wanted to

FANNY AND KATE.

make me do something that was wrong."

"You are not always so nice," sneered Fanny.

" I don't mean to do wrong, anyhow, as some folks do."

" Do you mean me ? "

" No matter whom I mean."

Fanny was so angry that she walked up to Kate and pulled her "shaker" down over her face. She also used some naughty words when she did so, which I will not repeat.

Kate, in her turn, was very angry with the saucy girl, and wanted to "pay" her for what she had done. But Fanny did not wait for any reply, and ran away just as fast as she could.

It would have been much better for Kate if she had let her go; but she was so angry she could not do this; she wanted to strike back again. Without thinking of the milk in the pail, she started to run after the naughty girl.

For a few moments she ran with all her might, and had nearly caught Fanny, when a stone tripped her up, and she fell upon the ground.

Then she thought of the milk, and tried to save it; but the cover of the kettle came off, and it was all spilled on the ground.

The fall did not hurt her, but the laugh with which her misfortune was greeted by Fanny roused a very wicked

3

spirit in her heart, and drop-
ping the pail, which she had
picked up, she pursued her.

But the naughty girl had
the start of her, and though
she followed her a good way
she could not overtake her.
Then she stopped in the path,
and cried with anger and
vexation. The thought of
the milk which had been
spilled, was, after all, the
worst part of the affair.

Walking back to the place

where the accident had happened, she picked up the pail again, and began to think what she should do. It was of no use now for her to go to Mrs. O'Brien's. She had no milk for the children's supper.

What would her mother say to her if she should return home and tell her she had spilled all the milk? She had told her to be careful, and she felt that she had been very careless.

It was not necessary that
she should chase the naughty
girl, whatever she said; and
she could not help seeing that
she had been very careless.
While she was thinking about
it, Ben Tinker came along.
He lived in the next house
to Mr. Lamb, and the children were well acquainted
with each other.

"What is the matter with
you, Kate?" asked Ben, when
he saw that her eyes were

red, and her face was wet with tears.

I have just spilled a pailful of milk on the ground," sobbed Kate.

"O, well, it's no use to cry for spilled milk," laughed Ben.

"I was carrying it to Mrs. O'Brien."

"No matter; she will get along very well without it."

"That ugly Fanny Flynn struck me on the head, and

that's what made me spill the milk."

" Didn't you hit her back ? "

" I couldn't catch her; she ran away. I was chasing her when I fell down and spilled the milk."

" You can catch her some time; when you do, give it to her."

But Kate had got over her anger, and heartily wished she had not attempted to catch Fanny. Besides, she very well knew that Ben was giving her bad advice.

That passage from the New Testament, "If any man smite thee on the one cheek, turn to him the other also," came to her mind, and she felt how wicked it was to harbor a desire for revenge.

The loss of the milk, and what would follow when she went home, gave her more trouble than the injury she had received from the naughty girl.

"I don't know what I shall do," said she, beginning to cry again, as she thought of her mother.

"Do? you can't do any thing — can you? The milk is gone, and all you have to do is to go home," replied Ben.

"What will my mother say?"

"No matter what she says, if she don't whip you or send you to bed without your supper."

"She won't whip me, and I have been to supper."

"Then what are you crying about?"

"Mother says I am very careless; and I know I am," whined Kate.

"Don't be a baby, Kate."

"I spoiled a flower this afternoon, and mother scolded me and shook me for it. She told me to be very careful with this milk, and now I have spilled the whole of it."

"Well, if you feel so bad, why need you tell her any thing about it?"

"About what?" asked Kate, looking up into his face, for she did not quite understand him.

"You needn't tell her you spilled the milk. She will never find it out."

"But she will ask me."

"What if she does? Can't you tell her you gave the milk to the old woman, and that she was very much obliged to her for sending it ?"

" I can do that," said Kate.

She did not like the plan, but it seemed to her just then that any thing would be better than telling her mother than she had spilled the milk ; and, wicked as it was, she resolved to do it.

CRYING FOR SPILLED MILK.

III.

KATE did not think of the poor woman and her hungry children when she made up her mind to tell her mother such a monstrous lie.

She did not think how very wicked it was to deceive her mother, just to escape, perhaps, a severe rebuke for her carelessness.

She felt all the time that

she was doing wrong, but she
tried so hard to cover it up,
that her conscience was not
permitted to do its whole
duty.

When we are tempted to
do wrong, something within
us tells us not to do it; but
we often struggle to get rid
of this feeling, and if we suc-
ceed the first time, it is easier
the next time. And the
more we do wrong, the easier
it becomes to put down the
little voice within us.

It was so with Kate. She had told falsehoods before, or it would not have been so easy for her to do it this time. If we do not take care of our consciences, as we do of our caps and bonnets, they are soon spoiled.

Did you ever notice that one of the wheels on your little wagon, when it becomes loose, soon wears out? The more it sags over on one side, the weaker it grows.

While the wheel stands up straight, it does not seem to wear out at all.

It is just so with your conscience — your power to tell right from wrong. While you keep it up straight, it works well, and never wears out. But when it gets a little out of order, it grows worse very fast, and is not of much more value than a lighthouse without any light in it.

Kate's conscience had begun to sag over on one side. It was growing weak, and did not remind her of her wrong deeds with force enough to make itself heeded. If she could only escape the reproof of her mother, she did not care.

Thus moved by the wicked counsel of Ben Tinker, she hastened home. She tried to look as if nothing had happened, but her eyes were still very red from crying; and her mother wanted to know what had made her cry.

" Fanny Flynn struck me, and pulled my 'shaker' over my face," replied Kate.

"What did she do that for ? "

" She asked me to give her a drink of the milk, and because I wouldn't, she struck me," answered Kate, placing her pail upon the kitchen table.

" She is a naughty girl, and

I will go and see her mother about it. What did she say to you?"

"She asked me for a drink of the milk."

"What did you answer?"

"I told her it was for Mrs. O'Brien's children, and that it wouldn't be right for me to give it to her, and I would not."

"Well, I will see to that. I think it is a pity if I can't send one of my children out

on an errand of charity without her being treated in this
manner.   She shall suffer for
it."

"She is a naughty girl,
mother; and I never mean
to speak to her again as long
as I live," said Kate, with
much apparent earnestness.

"You did right not to give
her any of the milk, and I
am glad you did not.   I am
happy that my daughter has
been brave enough to do

right, and even to suffer for doing it. You are a good girl, Kate."

"I meant to be, mother."

"What did Mrs. O'Brien say when you gave her the milk?" continued Mrs. Lamb.

"She said she was much obliged to you," replied Kate, not daring to look her mother in the face.

"Did you see the children?"

"Yes, mother."

Mrs. Lamb was going to ask more questions about the family, but something called her attention away, and Kate was saved from telling more falsehoods.

She took a book and tried to read, but she could not, for she did not feel like a good girl. The little voice within told her how wicked she had been, and she began to wish that she had not deceived her mother.

While she sat with the book in her hand, her father came home; and her mother told him what Fanny Flynn had done. He was very angry when he had heard the story, and asked Kate a great many questions about the affair.

"You did well, Kate," and I am glad you were so brave and so smart," said Mr. Lamb.

"Of course I could not

give her any of the milk when it was for the poor widow's hungry children."

"You did right, Kate," repeated her father. "The poor children might have had to go to bed hungry if you had given up the milk to that bad girl."

"I know it, father."

"Only think what a sad thing it would have been if the poor little ones had been sent hungry and crying to bed. That Fanny Flynn must be taken care of. When little girls get to be so bold as that, it is high time something was done."

"I think so, too, father."

"It is time for you to go to bed now, Kate," said her mother.

"I am ready, mother, for I am tired as I can be."

Kate was glad to get away from her father and mother, for while they were praising her for her good conduct, she knew very well that she did not deserve it.

What would her parents think if they knew that she had spilled all the milk on the ground? What would they say to her if they found out that she had told them so many lies?

The more she thought of her conduct, the more she felt that she had done wrong. She now saw that, if she had

returned home and told her
mother the truth, she would
have excused the fault, and
sent another pail of milk to
the poor sick woman's hungry
children.

She wished she had done
so, for it would have been a
great deal better to be scolded
for her carelessness than to
feel as guilty as she now felt.
She was sure that it was far
better to suffer a great deal
than to do even a little wrong.

She was not satisfied either
that her mother would have
scolded her, if she had stated
the whole truth to her — that
Fanny Flynn had made her
spill the milk.

She went to bed; but when
her mother bade her good
night, and took the lamp in
her hand, she begged her to
leave it, for she did not like
to be alone in the dark.

It seemed just as though a
wicked spirit was tormenting

her; and though she was in the habit of going to sleep without a light, the darkness was terrible to her at this time. She did not even wish to be left alone, but she dared not ask her mother to stay with her.

When Mrs. Lamb had gone out, Kate covered her face wholly under the bed-clothes, and shut her eyes as close as she could, trying in this manner to go to sleep.

But her guilty conscience gave her no rest.

Then she opened her eyes, and looked around the room; but every thing in the chamber seemed to mock and reproach her. Again and again she shut her eyes, and tried to sleep.

The little voice within would speak now, in the silence of her chamber. She had never felt so bad before; perhaps because she had never been so wicked before. Do you want to know why she suffered so much? It was because she could not keep from her mind those hungry, crying children.

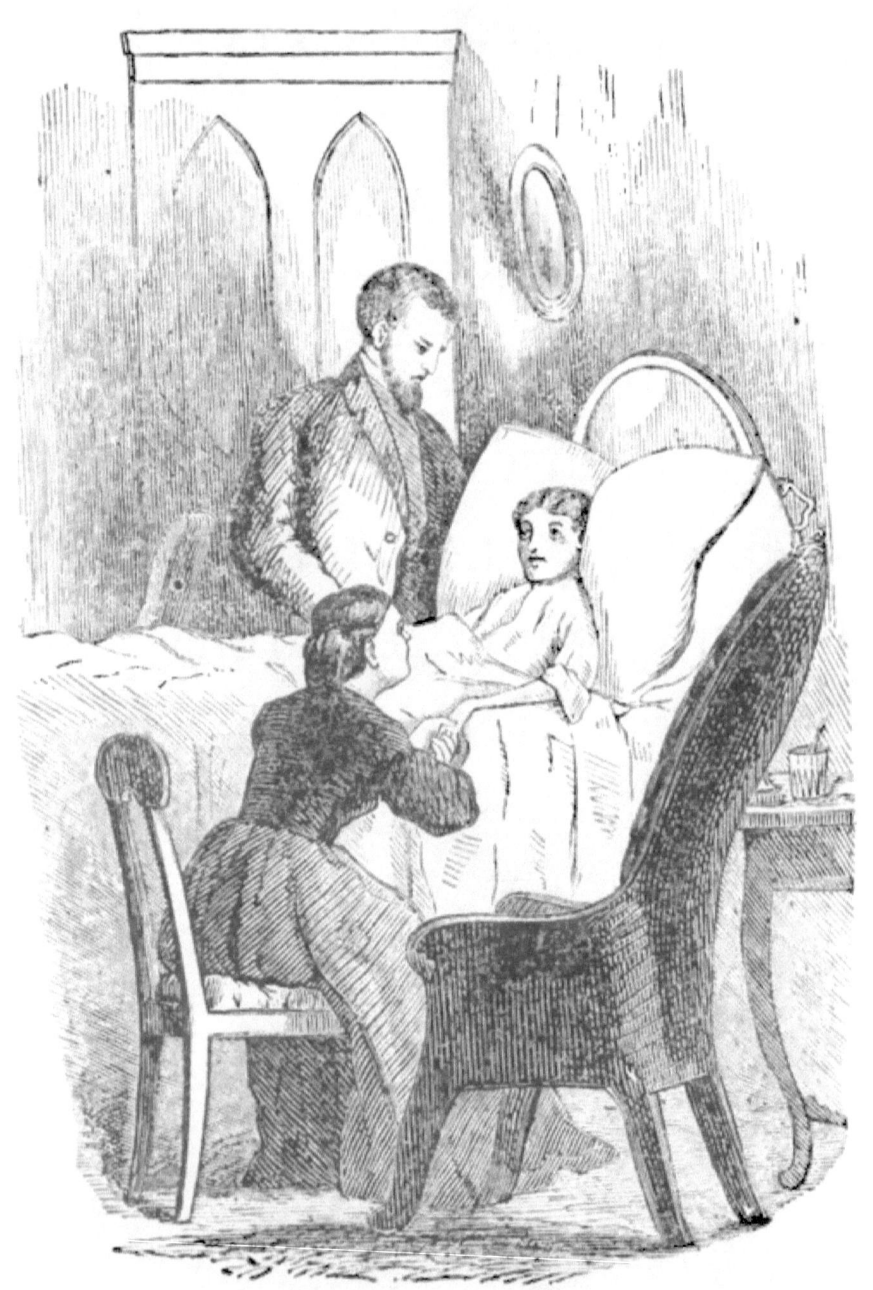

KATE TELLS THE WHOLE STORY.

IV.

Poor Kate! She had certainly never been so wicked in her life before. The words of her father still lingered in her ears, and she could almost hear the moans of those hungry, crying children.

She had never been sent to bed in her life without her supper, and it looked like a dreadful thing to her — perhaps even more dreadful than it really was.

If there had been nothing but the falsehoods she had told, she might have gone to sleep; but it was sad to think that she had deprived the poor children of their supper, and sent them hungry to bed. This seemed to be the most wicked part of her conduct.

I do not know how many times she turned over in the bed, nor how many times she pulled the clothes over her eyes to shut out the sad picture of those hungry and crying children that would come up before her, in spite of all she could do to prevent it.

She tried to think of other things — of the scene with Fanny; of her school; of a picnic party she had attended on the first of May; of almost every thing, indeed; but it did no good. The poor children could not be banished from her mind.

Kate had been sick with the measels, with the scarlet fever, and the mumps; and she remembered how bad she felt at these times; but it seemed to her now that she would rather have all these diseases at once than suffer from a guilty conscience.

When she was sick, her mother bent over her and pitied her, and did all she could to ease her pain; and even when she was burning with fever, and racked with pain, she felt happier than she did now.

She could not inform her mother how bad she felt, for that would expose her guilt. She heard the clock strike nine, and every moment appeared to her like an hour. Those poor little children constantly haunted her; whether her eyes were open or shut, still she saw them crying, and heard them moaning, and begging their sick mother to give them some supper.

O, Kate! how severely was she punished for the sin she had committed! Her mother and her father had praised her, but still she was unhappy.

Slowly, very slowly, the time passed away, and she heard the clock strike ten. She could endure her sufferings no longer; and she burst into tears, sobbing and moaning as if her heart would break.

For some time she cried; but as her distress increased, she sobbed and moaned so loud that her father and mother, who were in the adjoining room, heard her, and hastened into the room to find out what ailed her.

"What is the matter, my child?" anxiously asked her mother. "Haven't you been asleep since you went to bed?"

"No, mother," sobbed Kate.

"What ails you? Are you sick?"

"No, mother."

"What are you crying for, then?"

"O mother!"

"Why, what ails you, child? Have you been frightened?"

"No, mother."

"Tell us what ails you, Kate," added her father.

Both of her parents were

greatly alarmed about her, for they loved their little girl very much ; and they knew that something must ail her, or she would not have lain awake so long, or have cried so bitterly.

"Can't you tell us what ails you, Kate?" inquired her mother, very tenderly.

"I have been very naughty, mother," replied Kate, almost choking with emotion.

"Naughty, child?"

"Yes, mother."

"I thought you had been very good," added Mr. Lamb.

"No, I have not; I have been very wicked, and you will never forgive me."

"Why, what have you done, Kate? How strange you act, my child!"

"I can't help it, mother. If you will forgive me this time, I will never be so wicked again while I live."

"Tell us all about it, Kate,

and we will forgive you," said her father, very kindly.

The poor girl sobbed so that she could not speak for some time, for the tenderness of her parents made her feel a great deal worse than if they had scolded her severely.

"What have you done, Kate?" repeated Mrs. Lamb.

"I didn't carry the milk to Mrs. O'Brien, mother," gasped the poor penitent, as she uncovered her eyes, and looked up in the face of her parents to notice the effect of her confession upon them.

"Didn't carry it to her?" was the exclamation of her father and mother at the same time.

"No; I spilled it on the ground."

"Why, Kate! what did you do that for?"

"I couldn't help it — I mean I was careless. When Fanny Flynn struck me, I ran after her. My foot tripped, and I fell, and spilled all the milk."

"Why didn't you tell me so, Kate?"

"I didn't dare to tell you; I was afraid you would scold at me, as you did for spoiling the peony."

Kate felt a little better now that she had confessed her fault, and she was able to look her parents in the face.

"Why, Kate, if you had

only told me, I should not
have scolded you.   You may
have been careless, but it was
all the fault of Fanny Flynn."

"No, mother; I was care-
less.   I forgot all about the
milk, I was so angry."

"And so the poor children
had no supper, after all,"
added Mr. Lamb.

"O father! It was what
you said about them that
made me feel so bad. I am
sure I shall never be so very

wicked again.   Let me carry them some milk now."

"What are you talking about ?   It is after ten o'clock, my child."

"No matter, father ; I am not afraid to go in the dark, if I can only carry them their supper."

"No, no, Kate.   I will carry them the milk, though it is rather late, and probably they are all asleep by this time."

"But will you forgive me, father and mother?"

"Freely, my child; you have suffered severely already for your fault, and I hope it will be a lesson to you which will last as long as you live," said her father.

"It will," said Kate, earnestly.

Both her parents kissed her, in token of their forgiveness; and Mr. Lamb put on his coat, while Mrs. Lamb

went to the cellar for a pail of
milk, with which he soon left
the house on his errand of
kindness and charity.

Kate felt a great deal better then, and before her father
returned, she was fast asleep.
Mr. Lamb found the poor
woman still up.   The children had had bread and water, but no milk, for their supper, and she was very glad
to have some for them when
they waked up in the night.

And she was very grateful to Mr. Lamb for thinking of her at that hour, and thanked God for giving her such kind and thoughtful friends.

From that time, Kate was a better girl, and tried hard to reform her life and character. She tried so hard, and succeeded so well, that she very soon lost the name of " Careless Kate."

Mr. Lamb went to see Fanny Flynn's parents the

KATE A BETTER GIRL.

next day, and they promised
to punish her for her conduct.
After that Kate did not pro-
voke her, and they never had
any more trouble.

Now my readers have seen
that Kate's fault led her
into falsehood and deception,
which are worse than carelessness; and I hope they
will all learn to be careful
and truthful.

NOTHING TO DO.

"My kitty is purring
  Upon the hearth rug
Rolled up in a bundle
  Just like a great bug.
I wonder what kitty
  Is thinking about;
What makes her so happy
  I cannot find out.

"She has no hard lessons
  To bother her brain,

No spelling and reading
   To study in vain;
She ought to be happy
   With nothing to do
But play all the morning —
   And I should be, too."

Thus Nellie kept thinking,
   And spoke out her thought.
The words which she uttered
   Her mother's ear caught.
" You wish to be idle
   Like kitty, dear, there,
And play all the morning,
   Or sleep in your chair?"

"I don't like my lessons;

I think 'tis a pity

I can't be as happy

As dear little kitty.

That ugly old spelling

I never can learn!

O, into a kitty

I wish I could turn!"

"I am not a fairy,"

Her mother replied;

"To me all the power

Of magic's denied;

But you may be idle

From morning till night,

And see if 'do nothing'

Will set your case right."

"O, shall I do nothing
But play all day long,
And sing with my kitty
A holiday song?
How happy, and merry,
And joyous 'twill be
To have no hard lessons—
From study be free!"

"Do what will best please you;
Be idle all day;
Recite no more lessons;
Do nothing but play."
Then Nellie, rejoicing,
Flew out of the room;
Played *hide*, *horse*, and *dolly*,
And rode on the broom.

But long before dinner
  Poor Nell had "played out,"
And studied, and studied,
  And wandered about,
To find some new pleasure,
  Some game, or some play,
To use up the hours,
  And end that long day ; —

And long before evening
  Was cross as a bear —
Just like the McFlimsey
  With "nothing to wear."
And tired of nothing,
  And tired of play,
No day was so tedious
  As that idle day.

"O mother! my lessons
    I think I will get,
And then I can play
    As I never played yet.
I do not feel happy
    With nothing to do;
I cannot endure it
    Another day through."

"I thought so, my Nellie;
    To make your play sweet
You must work, and be useful
    To those whom you meet.
The idle are never
    So happy as they
Who work for themselves
    Or for others each day."